Book

Bernadette Cohen

AuthorHouse™
1663 Liberty Drive, Suite 200
Bloomington, IN 47403
www.authorhouse.com
Phone: 1-800-839-8640

AuthorHouse™ UK Ltd.
500 Avebury Boulevard
Central Milton Keynes, MK9 2BE
www.authorhouse.co.uk
Phone: 08001974150

© 2007 Bernadette Cohen. All rights reserved.

No part of this book may be reproduced, stored in a retrieval system, or transmitted by any means without the written permission of the author.

First published by AuthorHouse   7/9/2007

ISBN: 978-1-4259-7870-9 (sc)

Printed in the United States of America
Bloomington, Indiana

This book is printed on acid-free paper.

For my nieces Victoria, Sophie and Phoebe.

Much thanks and acknowledgement to my editor Stephen Farrant. Much thanks and acknowledgement to the Bright Agency for providing the illustrator Michael Garton.

Table of Contents

Book	1
Books New Home	7
The Spirit Queen	15
Travelling	20
Enlightenment	44
Farewell	48
Finally Home	50

Book

The early morning sun shines in through the tall library windows casting warm shadows on the books. Book was feeling sad and fed up. Would the children come today? She needed to hear their voices and was beginning to feel lonely. Book was tired of just sitting on the bookshelf with the other storybooks. She did not need to take a nap in the afternoon like the baby books or the older books, no her mind was far too busy deep in thought. No, she wanted an adventure but Book knew this could only happen if she were chosen and read. The Three Witches and the BFG had adventures and so did that clever Mr Wolf, Book wanted something to happen in her life. Suddenly she could hear the children's voices getting louder and louder, "Oh please choose me" Book thought, she waited and waited but nothing happened. She sat on the bookshelf listening to other books adventures. Tears began to cloud her eyes and roll down her cheeks , she felt so desperately bored, sad, and alone, but just at that moment something did happen, she felt herself being lifted up, up into the air and finally off of that dusty old bookshelf. "Oooh I've finally been chosen, anyway it was about time those children wised up to the really wicked stories round here," Book murmured into the air.

But instead of being taken to the teacher Book began to feel something wet and bristly on her coat, "Oh no I don't believe it, it couldn't possibly be that I wouldn't be treated in that manner, I'm far too beautiful and exciting no no no not that." But her biggest nightmare had come true, she was being sucked into by a child. She felt disgusted, enough is enough she thought, as soon as I'm put back on the bookshelf I'll think of a plan of how to get out of this place. Book began to cry even more , I'm so unhappy and forgotten about, I feel so useless and unloved, the only time I seem to be remembered is when a child gets hungry and sucks on me instead of sweets or chips, at least sweets and chips are loved. Book began to sob and sob as the child placed her back on to the bookshelf. Whilst crying she felt herself again being lifted up into the air she was now almost past caring until she fully realised what was happening and the shame of it all. She could feel herself becoming dizzier and dizzier, then very travel sick "oh no" instead of being read she was being thrown around the library, the children were playing catch with her as if she were a ball. Then everything went dark as she felt herself falling down, down, down. Oh where Oh where was she now?

Book looked around her she had been thrown down in a dark corner where it seemed as she squinted around her all the old worn torn books of the library lived. The dreaded corner that all the books called, the waiting to die corner. Book could not bare it, why you only had to look at her coat to see she did not belong there. Book gazed around her, enclosing her on all sides were worn, torn old books. How could Book have a conversation with them, some of them looked so very old. The words safe, wicked and cool most probably had different meanings to them, Book was at a complete loss and her back began to give her terrible pain. She thought desperately please, please somebody come and rescue me. Just at that moment she heard the librarian's voice becoming louder and louder, Book had never got used to her voice it was so harsh and shrill.

In Stoke Newington the librarian's voice had been so warm and friendly, how things had changed thought Book. Whenever this librarian was close by she felt a cold shudder, she felt one now. "For instance take this book", once again Book felt herself being lifted up into the air and her back being pushed, the pain was just too awful. "As you can see" the librarian continued "the spine of this book is almost broken."

The librarian then placed the book down amongst all the old worn, torn broken books. Book felt the tears rising she began to cry and cry. Oh please, please she thought desperately somebody, anybody come and rescue me. The next morning rubbing her eyes, Book heard the big key being turned in the lock, the librarian had arrived. Book looked around her utterly dismayed she sank down low into that damp dark corner. The afternoon came and brought with it the children and their teacher but Book was no longer housed alongside the storybooks on the library bookshelf and so had no chance of being chosen. The afternoon passed by so slowly and the evening followed bringing with it darkness, Book knew another talk free lonely night was on its way. What she hated most was not the darkness it had only become dark because the sun had gone to bed, well that's what one of the Three Little Pigs had told her. No her main problem when it became dark and night fell was the utter loneliness, at least on the story bookshelf the books talked together.

Now where she was nobody talked to one and another. There was a deadly silence amongst all the books; no life was to be had there in that damp corner. The next morning Book heard the sound of the key being turned in the lock and recognised the quick marching footsteps of the librarian, again Book had to listen to other books adventures as the day very slowly turned and the light faded once again. The next morning Book awoke feeling very depressed the dark night seemed to endlessly go on forever and ever, then suddenly she heard a voice very close by. Book straightened herself up from her sunken pose feeling a dull aching in her back as she did so. This voice was not the voice of the librarian, it was a soft voice but not a voice she recognised. It had youthfulness and spirit in it, no it was definitely not the voice of the librarian, I've got it Book thought, it's that young library assistants voice. "What about books like these, it's such a great shame to let them go to waste. All they need is a quick repair job and we could sell them." Book felt herself being lifted up into the air and her back being pushed. Her spine was being repaired with sticky tape, it hurt but she knew the pain was worth it if it meant getting away from that dreadful corner. After the repair job she was placed on a big wooden table in the hall.

Gazing to the right of her the books spine read The Hungry Caterpillar, she then asked The Hungry Caterpillar why they were there? "Oh don't you know the good news we have the chance of being bought by a child and given a home," in fact he went on to tell book how privileged the story books were on that table. "We are the most sought after books here, way over there on that smaller table those non story books sell for 10p, we sell for 20p." These last words made Book feel much better. "About time I was given recognition around here" Book mumbled into the air. "Of course it really depends on who buys you," said The Hungry Caterpillar, "it could be a kind child or a really nasty child." Poor James and the Giant Peach", continued The Hungry Caterpillar, "I heard from Georges Marvellous Medicine that James was bought by a really cruel owner, he ended up being used as firewood in the end". Book began to worry, what if she was bought by a really cruel owner, "Oh I do hope I'm bought by a kind child" Book softly murmured into the air. Just then she heard the last of the children's voices, then a gloominess of darkness began to creep in through the tall library windows. Suddenly Book heard voices very close by, they were children's voices and they were laughing. Next Book felt herself being lifted into the air by the hands of a child who then called "come on Timothy look at this story book with me". Book was finally being read, she started to feel so happy but all of a sudden the child's voice began to change and grow angry. "I hate reading books especially story books I really detest them" said the little girl. Then Book started feeling dizzy she could feel herself falling down, down, down, she landed on her now weak spine with a great thud and immediately felt this shooting pain in her back. The little girl laughed as she cruelly began to tear into Book's pages. Then Book began to feel so hot, she struggled to breathe as all around her choking fiery hot flames encased her. The fiery red flames were stabbing into her body like hundreds and hundreds of red hot daggers all over her piercing into her and so much smoke. Her torn body had been placed on the fire she was going to die and then everything went black.

The morning light shone in through the tall library windows, rubbing her eyes Book looked around her she was back in the library amongst all the other books for sale, it had all been a nightmare dream. She shuddered when she thought of that burning hot fire and those cruel children. The morning seemed to last forever again, Book began to feel bored, when afternoon came she began to feel sleepy but just then she heard children's voices close by. "Hey Brendan come and look at this story book with me and the pictures look", book felt so proud she began to feel a lump in her throat. Bernadette lifted Book gently in her hands and began turning Books pages to show her brother. Book knew she was in the right hands she could feel it, please buy me and take me home with you Book thought, "lets ask Mummy if she will buy it for us" said Bernadette. When book heard this she could hardly contain her excitement, "Mummy, mummy can you buy this book for Brendan and me its only 20 pence". "I'll just see if I have 20 pence in my purse" said mum, "yes your in luck here we are." Bernadette took the twenty pence to the librarian holding Book firmly in her hand, tears of joy flowed down Books face she was finally about to be read and go to a nice home.

Books New Home

After the car journey Book had been carried into the house by Bernadette and placed on a soft cushion in the lounge. Book began to look at her new surroundings. Over in the far corner were books and lots of them on a light wooden bookshelf. In fact it was a very light looking room, Book had got quite used to damp dark rooms until now. She looked back again at the books all though it was nice to come home to such a familiar sight, she had been more than just a little worried on the journey in the car, now she felt relaxed and secure. Just then the girl Bernadette came back into the room. Book felt herself being transported gently through the air and brought down again onto the childs knees Book was then opened.

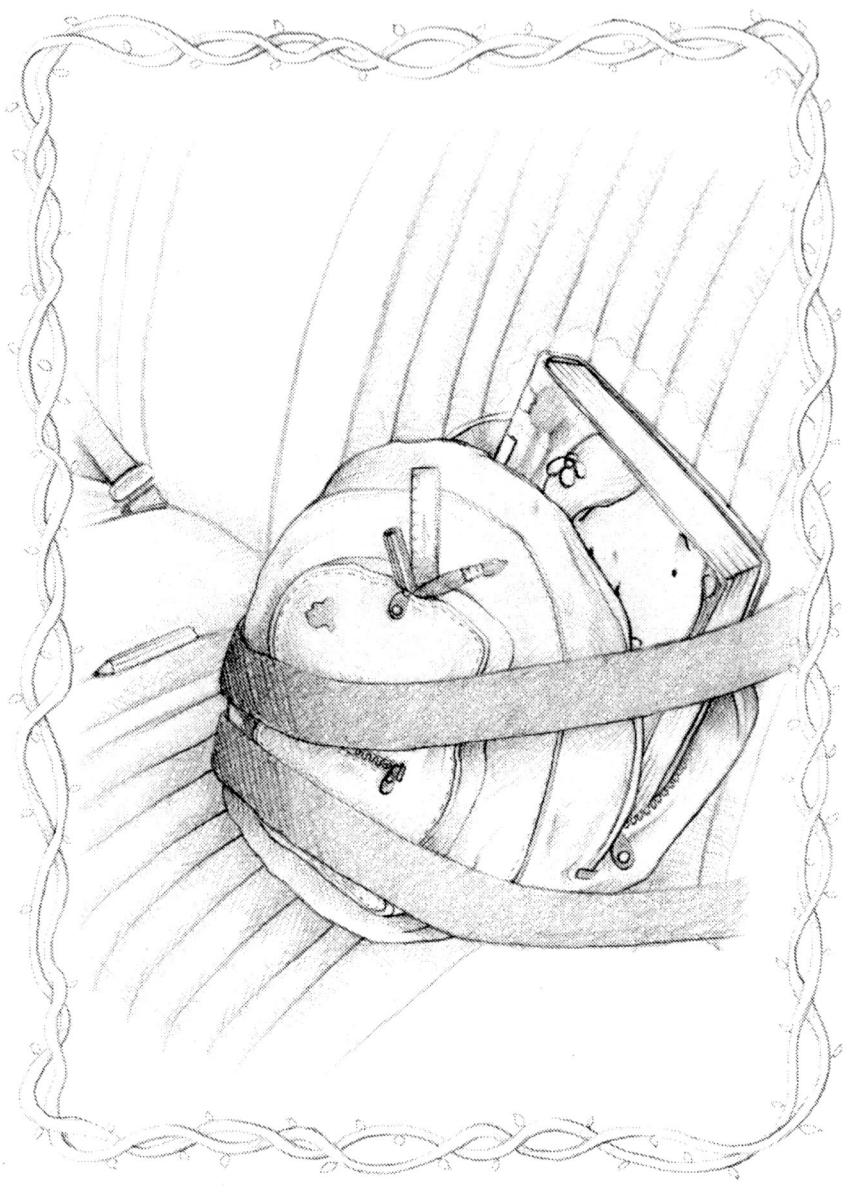

Book felt so happy as she started to feel of use once again, slowly she felt the life coming back into her body as her pages were turned and the warm sun shone down upon her. In days passed the long hours with nothing to do in the library had been spent being extremely bored or sleeping, so many days wasted in this way and most of all never being read. She had almost forgotten what it was to be a book, she had just about reached breaking point when the children found and rescued her. Now she could feel the warm sun on her and a kind child browsing her pages "Bernadette, Bernadette" a womens voice called, I wonder who that is?. Book thought, as time flowed on she found out it was Bernadette's mother, Bernadette hurriedly placed the book back on the bookshelf.

Book wasn't there for very long before she heard a cough followed by another cough then another. Book looked down the bookshelf no coughs there and then turning her head to look the other way she came to the book that had been coughing. "Good afternoon" they didn't wait for a reply they just carried on talking "I'm very pleased to meet you and you no doubt will be very pleased to meet me when I tell you who I am". Apart from the confidence of the speaker the fact of the matter was that the book looked so plain and threadbare, in truth their coat was completely naked! "May I introduce myself dear lady", before Book could answer they carried on "I am the one the honourable adored by all, magnificent Emperor, the rest of my title is immaterial dear lady. I always say it's not what life throws at you, it all comes down to how you see things. Being in a comfortable position or having lots of money does not make life easier not that I have ever had the misfortune to live like a pauper. It's just the way you see things dear lady and I see things just right". The Emperor however was clearly in a world of his own for he just kept on repeating "it's just the way you see things, it is just the way you see things." Book left him alone for it was quite obvious that The Emperor had no need of another book with which to converse.

Looking on further down the line for some company book came across a brightly coloured coat. "How do you do I'm Gulliver from Gulliver's Travels I noticed you having a chat with The Emperor, well if you can call it that he does like the sound of his own voice and then the matter of his coat! You get used to his voice after a while chatting and chatting about the same old thing, how you see things. I suppose he didn't mention the nights around here by any chance?"

"No" said book. Gulliver carried on "well when darkness begins to unfold around us and the peoples are making their ways to their beds that's when us books really come to life. We have a right old party of conversations and entertainment, the fireworks really go off some nights."

Just then the children came back into the room Gulliver was quiet. Book felt herself being lifted up into the air and recognised the gentle way in which she was being handled, she was placed on the girl's knees and opened. There was a peaceful silence in the air as the girl looked into the pages, "Hey Brendan come and look at this book we bought from the library, see how the green mist starts to move as you look into the picture." "Your daydreaming again Bernadette you know what mum said and the teachers at school about your daydreaming and how it nearly always gets you into trouble, hey lets go and play outside."

"okay", said Bernadette as she carefully placed Book back on the bookshelf.

Book felt so good it was ages and ages since she had really been brought back to life, this young girl had brought Book back to life again and Book felt so so happy. Like the Emperor had said it really was how you saw things and the young girl saw things just right. Book stopped thinking for a moment as she gazed down the left side of the bookshelf then down the right The Emperor, Gulliver and all the other books were taking an afternoon nap. Book felt she could now join them she hadn't felt so at home or relaxed like this ever. Book now understood the need for an afternoon nap she now needed the energy for on waking she may be required reading material and then there was the night time conversations to look forward to. Yes she certainly needed a nap to recharge her batteries, in the library she had felt afternoon napping pointless for she was never ever brought to life and read. Book closed her eyes and fell into a deep sleep. Book was awoken by the noises of human life she looked in front of her, Bernadette and Brendan were watching television the noise from the television disturbed Books thinking, normally she didn't notice it but now she eagerly awaited for the lounge to become the books domain, hopefully the children would stop watching television soon and go up to bed. Just then Book heard one of the children's voice's "Or you can play on the other game Bernadette", said Brendan "Come on lets go upstairs," he stood in the doorway to leave the lounge, Book let out a sigh of relief as Bernadette reached over and switched the television off. They left the lounge and climbing the stairs you could hear mothers voice call "You're not to stay on that computer all night Brendan a few games and then go to bed, Brendan do you hear me."

"Yes mother" came the joint reply.

Book looked into the room, darkness had begun to unfold around her, then she heard a distinct cough on her right, she looked down the bookshelf and noticed The Emperor was awake and looking right in Books direction. "Good evening how was your morning nap?" The Emperor didn't wait for a reply, he just carried on talking. "Well I've been in all the best places, I expect you can see that by the exquisite materials on my coat." The truth was as before The Emperor's coat was completely plain, naked and threadbare, Book decided not to comment and left The Emperor talking. "It was when the tailors came to first see me at a very high price visit, well as I'm sure you are aware the more expensive the tailors the more expensive the materials are, and the more valuable the higher the price, so naturally only the highest highest prices would suit a person of my standing naturally," "naturally" book replied. The Emperor continued talking, "they clothed me in exquisitely refined materials beautiful rich fabrics suited for a special royal highly regarded person as my self," Book looked again at The Emperor's coat and again saw a colourless plain threadbare coat, Book thought the Emperor blind? Of course he was blind to his own ego and his ego had become so dominant a feature of his character it now blinded him to the truth The Emperor then continued "You see its all a matter of how you see things my dear lady, its just the way you see things" repeated the Emperor.

Book left the Emperor talking to himself she looked further on down the bookshelf and came to a very old looking book judging by the faded worn coat, it had obviously spent many years in this world.

"Oh hello I'm Bedouin much travelled in my time" "I thought as much when I looked at your coat" said Book, Bedouin continued "Yes although I grew up in the British Library I was eventually sent to a local library then farmed out, a Greek family bought me, such fun I had in their house, such an academic family, the history of maths being my favourite subject. I had such a knowledgeable time in that house, then the Greek wife gave me to Bernadette's mother and now I'm here and happy to be amongst such jovial company for I was becoming a little lonely with the Greek family as time passed on. Anyways I must stop chatting now as it's the books evening entertainment period" Book then looked along the shelf until she came to Gulliver who was silent and waiting like the other books on the bookshelf. "Do you like music?" Gulliver asked Book, "We have a songbook on the shelf that's what all of us books are waiting for, Voices nightly show. I'll introduce you to her and I'm sure if I ask her for a request she'll oblige me." Gulliver asked Voices if she would mind singing a special song for the new arrival. "Why certainly it would be a pleasure" crooned Voices. Her voice was certainly pleasurable but it was not a song Book recognised, the song was, She's only a bird in a guilded cage, Book definitely had never heard of it. It must have been before Books time because Voices had never heard of Boyzone and electronic music was beyond her. Voices said just as the birds made music so did she. She did have a beautiful voice its just that Book didn't recognise any of the songs, no matter thought Book each of her songs was like a story. Listening to Voices, Books eyes began to feel heavy, with Voices songs echoing in her ears she fell asleep.

The Spirit Queen

Morning came and Book gazed out of the tall lounge window onto the garden. A linnet had just flown out of a sky of blue onto a branch of an old oak tree that stood tall and proud in a corner of the garden. The linnet took rest on the branch, gazed around her before awakening the world with her morning song. Book had fallen asleep to Voices songs the night before now she was awakened by the songbird as she sang so sweetly. Book took a slow deep breath breathing in all the goodness that the morning had brought. It really was a wonderful morning it certainly wasn't like waking up in that library with that damp dusty smell in the air. She remembered how she had been treated, played catch with then being thrown down into that damp dark corner that all the books called, the waiting to die corner and then that dark horrible horrible nightmare where she had been burnt alive. She took another deep breath, she was so relieved to be free of such dreadful times, she felt so very lucky as she gazed out of the lounge window and listened to the birds morning song. Book now heard somebody on the stairs the family must be up, she gazed down the rightside of the bookshelf The Emperor was still dozing she gazed further on down Gulliver was still sleeping. Oh well Book thought I may as well entertain myself and read my own tales but just then she heard somebody at the lounge door. It was the young girl, now this girl had the spirit but she didn't know it yet. Bernadette walked over to the bookshelf leaning forward and reaching up, Book felt herself being lifted into the air and then brought down to rest on the knees of the young girl, Book pages were opened.

As Bernadette began to leaf through Books pages she came to the picture of the dense green forest, her eyes became transfixed she stared and stared into the forest. Her eyes then fixed on the words, **THE GREEN MIST IS IN THE AIR THE CHILDS FACE IS PALE AND FAIR, THE SPIRIT QUEEN CANNOT BE FOUND WHILE THE MIST LAYS ON THE GROUND,** as Bernadette read these words they began to lift off the page of the Book floating out into the air. The words echoed again and again in Bernadette's mind, she began to feel lightheaded and dizzy. Green mist began to rise from the page of the Book and Bernadette's eyelids began to feel heavy, try as she might she could not keep them open, the Book fell from her hands onto the floor. When she awoke she was no longer at home but in a green dense forest, she could feel a cool breeze on her cheeks as it danced through the branches of the trees and the faint cry of somebody calling. It called**," turn around look on the ground"** then the faint voice called again. Bernadette looked for the voice but all she could see in front of her was a green dense mist on the ground and trees. She turned in the other direction but again it was the same, a green mist carpeted the forest floor and again more trees.

Bernadette stood still and began thinking, then Bernadette remembered yes it must be something to do with those last words in the Book now what were they? She put her thinking cap back on again. She began to remember placing together the words in the Book the something….something cannot be found while the mist lays on the ground she nearly had all of it, now what was that something something yes I've got it she then spoke out loudly **"the Spirit Queen cannot be found while the mist lays on the ground."** Finished, Bernadette stood and watched as all around her the green mist started to rise, float up into the air and then fade away. Then she saw something right by her shoe, it was the tiniest weaniest toadstall Bernadette had ever seen, as Bernadette stared at it, it began to glow and glow. At first she felt scared until she heard the soft gentle voice that seemed to be coming from the toadstall, it was then as she bent down lower she saw the Spirit

Queen. She was so tiny and fragile looking, she had Auburn hair that flowed right down to her feet and such sparkling green eyes. Her skin was like porcelain so very white and her green eyes began to sparkle as she spoke, she told Bernadette she had been sitting on that toadstall all the time Bernadette was in the forest. Then she told Bernadette it was only when she began to repeat the words from the Book that the green mist was able to rise and the Spirit Queen come to life. The young girl lowered her head to get closer and as she did so the Spirit Queen stretched out her tiny arms as if to embrace Bernadette. The Spirit Queen spoke "You have been called to the spirit world for a very important reason I am the Spirit Queen, head of all the spirits in the spirit world, spirits live inside story books and inside special people, you Bernadette possess the spirit but you don't know how to use it. You have been called to this place Bernadette in the hope that meeting me you will help the spirit world, story books and yourself. Bernadette it was your spirit that directed you to buy Book in the first place, the book you have bought holds magic powers. It is your spirit that drives you to find the story books you find. Spirits cannot live without story books and story books cannot live without being brought to life and read.

Everytime a story is read a spirit is brought to life. What is taking place in your world is very frightening and a great danger to the spirit and the story book world. We watched the arrival of the computer age, we are pleased with the important jobs computers are doing yet our earliest fears seem to be coming true. Story books no longer play as big a part in a child's life as they used to, storytellers hardly exist now and children seem to spend most of their lives on computers while story books gather dust on the bookshelves. Now not often will a child experience turning the pages of a book, of feeling and holding a book in ones hands. The computer cannot replace these experiences, computers may function fine under instruction but let us not forget they have no imagination, just think of the world without imagination. The computer cannot introduce the mind into the world of Never Never land where children learn to fly or travel with Gulliver to the land of The Little People or to meet with The BFG. Stories are the lifeblood of the people, if story reading continues at the rate it has been us spirits will surely die. As I have told you Bernadette spirits do not only live inside story books they also live inside special people, Bernadette you possess the spirit, you inherited it from your grandmother and now I need to teach you how to find your spirit. Close your eyes and clear your mind of all thoughts and let the spirit flow through your body and mind, concentrate on your spirit, feel it and listen to your body, let your spirit take over and fill up your whole body, your whole mind."

At first nothing happened then gradually Bernadette noticed warmth all over her body as she could hear the Spirit Queens voice telling her to focus on her body spirit, to listen to it and to let her body lead her. Her body began to feel so light she felt like she was floating, floating in the air, then she felt a tingling in her hands and feet. The Spirit Queen called out to her softly "Bernadette you can help the spirit world to be strong again" the Spirit Queen's voice echoed and echoed through Bernadette's mind until it became fainter and fainter and then stopped. When Bernadette opened her eyes the Spirit Queen had gone and the green mist began to grow thicker and thicker all around, Bernadette began to feel sleepy her eyelids very heavy they began to close. When she awoke she found herself back in the lounge at home. Book was lying at her feet she must have fallen asleep but what of the Spirit Queen and the spirit world? She began to wonder if it had all been a dream but just then she got the feeling of warmth all over her, her feet and hands began to tingle and her body to feel so light and floaty. It was then she knew she was not alone. Sitting in the lounge Bernadette could hear her mother's voice calling her, Bernadette's mother wanted to take Brendan and Bernadette shopping, Bernadette got up and left the lounge. The afternoon passed and the children returned with their mother from shopping. Brendan entered the lounge calling out "Bernadette it's your turn to make the supper I did it last week and make sure you put out those yummy chocolate muffins"okay" Came the reply.

Travelling

They all had supper in the kitchen then came in the lounge to play cards. They played rumi Brendan's favourite game but what was strange was Bernadette was winning every hand. Mum and Brendan were totally surprised when Bernadette again won the fourth game but they kept their thoughts to themselves until Bernadette again won the fifth game, it wasn't just that she won, it was the speed at which she won. As soon as Bernadette picked up her cards for the fifth game, no sooner did she have them in her hands then she was laying them down again, she did not have to rearrange the cards into any order for as soon as she picked them up she won hands down and won with the same cards but this time it was a different suit but again the same cards a 6, a 7, an 8, a 9, a 10, a jack and a Queen of hearts. This time Brendan had to say something "Bernadette you must have a jinx or some sort of spirit guiding you or you're a magician tonight with the cards." After the very strange card game everyone watched television then the children went up to bed. Night passed and with the darkness fading the dawn light shone in through the lounge windows.

Book heard the linnet's morning song as she gazed out of the lounge window onto the gardens. She had been in her home one full year now, in that time she had gotten to know all the books on the bookshelf. Bedouin had made a big impression on her in fact she idolised him and whenever he spoke Book made sure a respectable silence was given by all the books. In some ways he was a sort of father figure being male and of mature age, she had never known her real father, he was taken out of the library one day and never returned. She missed him very much especially when he would tell a night story. She also missed the story of how he told her a book was made, that's why she found Bedouin so interesting because he was never short of a story to tell and so she was in awe of him and hoped she would be as fluent a story teller when she grew older.

The Emperor had become an associate Gulliver and Voices good friends. Book heard noises on the stairs and guessed the family must be up for breakfast. After the family had breakfasted Bernadette began clearing away the breakfast things, Brendan went upstairs to have a shower and mother began work on her computer in her bedroom, come office. Since the passing away of her husband she earned extra monies working from home making up slogans for advertising companies. Bernadette left the kitchen having cleared away the breakfast things and now entered into the lounge sat down in the green chair and gazed out of the lounge windows onto the garden. She had taken to doing this ever since her adventure in the forest where she had met the Spirit Queen. Now she found that by spending time quietly in the green chair and concentrating just like the Spirit Queen had shown her in the forest on that day now she could feel her spirit. She felt so happy because now she was never alone. It had been hard when dad had died the year before, being and feeling so alone. It must have been really hard for mum, mum and dad being so close and doing everything together. Brendan found it really hard without dad, no more tussles or Saturday football practice.

Bernadette cleared her mind andreturned to concentrating on her body, she could feel her body getting lighter and lighter. She remembered that the Spirit Queen had told her it was very important to clear the mind fully of all thoughts for only then could the spirit enter the body. Just at that moment Bernadette's mother called to her, Bernadette rose and left the lounge.

Book looked along the bookshelf and realised the other books were waking. Before long The Emperor was awake and in full flow of conversation even though there was nobody to whom he was talking to but Book had grown quite accustomed to The Emperor's ways. There was somebody at the lounge door, this time it was Brendan he entered the lounge put the television on then sat down in the green chair. He put on the television whenever there was an opportunity, in fact Brendan would sit and watch television all day if it wasn't for Bernadette's intervention, Bernadette would simply walk into the room bemoan Brendan for watching television all the time and press the button. Brendan had given up the struggle long ago, Bernadette had always won with Mothers support. Bernadette and mother had named Brendan TV DOG. Just at this moment his sister entered the lounge "Brendan what have I told you about catching square eyes there we are I just press the button and it's done." Book felt quite contented with the girl's actions now the room was filled with peacefulness. Now that the television was off Brendan got up and walked through the lounge towards the door telling Bernadette he was going out into the garden to play football and asked Bernadette would she be goalie "okay" Bernadette replied, Bernadette left the lounge with Brendan. After a few games as goalie Bernadette told Brendan she had had enough and left Brendan playing in the garden and went back inside. She went into the lounge went over to the bookshelf reached up for Book brought her down and walked over to the green chair, she sat down placed Book on her lap and opened Books pages.

As if the Book knew Bernadette's thoughts it opened up onto the page where she had been last time. Immediately on looking at the page the green mist seemed to rise from the page and the forest trees seemed to be pulling. Bernadette could feel their branches reaching out to her and pulling her pulling her into the forest of green mist. Her eyelids began to feel so heavy they began to close. When Bernadette awoke this time she found herself in an old derelict house that smelt awful, a smell that made Bernadette feel quite sick. Bernadette looked around her this house looked as if it had been abandoned, everything was rotten in the dim light. In the hall Bernadette could see rotting fruit in the fruit bowl on the hall table so this was the smell but also a horrible musty dampness filled the air. As Bernadette stood there in this damp cold air she could hear the sobbing of a young child she stood still and listened again, yes it was definitely the cries of a young child. She looked ahead of her into the bare rooms downstairs and listened again, the cries were coming from above, upstairs. Ahead of her stood an old wooden staircase as she came closer she could see steps missing and the ones that were still intact looked thoroughly rotten. Bracing herself as she stood at the bottom of the staircase she began to shiver as the air around her grew much colder. Then something very very strange happened, as Bernadette's breath came out of her mouth it turned grey in the air then began to form grey clouds that sat motionless around her. When she placed her foot on the first step of the staircase these small grey clouds had joined together to form a veil of mist, Bernadette could hardly see anything ahead of her now. It had all become so very dangerous yet Bernadette could still hear the child's crying, the child's cries now echoed around the walls of the house. Bernadette's body followed the cries, her eyes but mainly her feet leading her, trembling and scared she climbed slowly on up the staircase.

A loud bang made Bernadette jump she nearly lost her footing lshe looked over the banister to the dark misty corner below, a black cat crept out looked at Bernadette and was gone. The childs voice continued to fill the air it sounded so sad, Bernadette had to get to it. The veil of mist seemed to be clearing as Bernadette continued climbing the staircase although she still had to climb very slowly as each step was treacherously creaky and sometimes when she raised her leg the step was missing so slowly she would raise it even higher to the next one, thank goodness she could almost see clearly ahead of her now. She finally reached the top and found herself on a small landing. Ahead of her were two wooden doors and either side of her were two more doors. She stood and listened and yes the child's sobbing was coming from one of the doors ahead of her, the one on the right. As she approached the child's sobbing stopped. Bernadette felt nervous her stomach began to churn, she stood for a moment and tried to get a grip on herself, whatever voice lay beyond that door whatever she may find she did not want to enter showing fear. She pushed open the door, it creaked loudly it was just about still hanging on the hinges. When she entered the room there huddled up in the corner was a small boy. As she approached him the small boy curled into a ball hugging himself as he wrapped his arms around his body. Bernadette came towards the small frightened child very slowly, "Hello my names Bernadette's what's yours?" The little boy unfolded his arms and stared at her. "It's alright you know," said Bernadette "I just heard your cries and came to find out if you were alright." The little boy continued to stare out at Bernadette. Bernadette repeated again "Look it's alright you know I've got a younger brother called Brendan and he has got red hair just like you." After a time of staring at Bernadette the little boy spoke, "I used to live here with my parents now their gone dead""Tell me more if you want" said Bernadette.

The little boy gazed into the room and then carried on talking "they all died in a car crash and I went to live with foster parents but I was so unhappy I came back to this house. It was not that my foster parents weren't kind they were but it's just that they didn't understand, at my foster parent's house there were no books to read, I felt really alone. Mummy bought me The BFG for my birthday I loved The Big Friendly Giant he was my best friend, I took him to my foster parents house and used to take him to bed but my foster mum said I should now forget about these silly books and use my mind for better things, but I missed my friend."

"Well" said Bernadette "you can come back to my house if you like, on our shelves there are lots of books and there is one book you may find very magical." The little boy listened studying Bernadette all the while and as he listened his eyes finally came to rest on Bernadette's blue eyes he gazed into them intently and began to feel safe. He then stood up walked over to her and took her hand. Bernadette explained

that they would have to tread very carefully on the stair floorboards as many of the boards were very rotten or missing and extremely dangerous, then she thought it used to be his home. Just as Bernadette thought the little boy turned to her at the top of the stairs and said "follow me I will lead us I know best" Bernadette followed carefully. Finally they reached the bottom step and were in the hall, they both walked to the front door then the little boy held her hand tighter as she opened i.

Bernadette gasped as she looked ahead of them, in front of them was a gianormous stripy balloon which seemed to fill the whole landscape. Suddenly a voice from the sky called out "Climb into the balloon and soon the childs teardrops will dry as you reach the sky," then followed only the sound of the wind whistling.

Bernadette still holding the little boys hand turned to him and said "Trust me I'll look after you lets climb into the balloon." As soon as they were safely in the basket the balloon took to the air, higher and higher they climbed into an ocean of blue sky. As the balloon began to climb higher and higher they heard the voice again **"Look out into the blue sky let your minds relax then your imaginations will grow."** They both turned looked at each other then looked out into a never ending land of blue where white fluffy clouds that looked like cotton wool balls drifted slowly by. Then they both gasped for there was the BFG, Tinkerbell and Peter Pan. Next appeared this bright light in the sky that began to form a circle of light and enclosed within was the Spirit Queen. The little boy began to laugh and cuddle Bernadette. Then just as suddenly as they had appeared The BFG, Tinkerbell and Peter Pan were gone, the bright circle of light remained but now it was empty the Spirit Queen had disappeared also. The little boy turned to Bernadette and asked "What's happened where have they gone?" Bernadette could hear a voice coming from the circle of light she turned to the little boy and said "Listen, listen there is a voice telling us something." The little boy stopped and listened Bernadette then began to recognise the voice it was the Spirit Queens.**"The books are not dead, you have seen their spirits roaming endlessly in the sky, why because the books are not opened and read, the spirit of the book world is destined to die but**

Bernadette you have been chosen, without your help the books and the spirit world will die." Then the voice was gone and just as the balloon had risen now it descended. When the balloon landed Bernadette and the boy climbed out, Bernadette turned and looking back to her utter astonishment the balloon and the little boy had vanished. Then Bernadette could feel her body growing very very tired, her eyelids grew heavy and began to close.

Through the darkness she could here a voice calling her, Bernadette. Bernadette opened her eyes it was her mothers voice calling "Bernadette Bernadette, I've been calling you for ages now and I've had to come out of the kitchen for you, well come on daydreamer I need you, you've been sleeping in that chair for goodness knows how long with that book on your lap.Put the book back on the shelf and come into the kitchen I need your help." Bernadette wanted to tell her mother all the time that she had visited an old derelict house where inside she had met a small boy and that both of them had gone for a ride in a big stripy balloon and in the sky had seen characters from books and met the Spirit Queen. In fact Bernadette wanted to share with her mother everything that had happened to her since they had brought Book back from the library but she knew it would be of no use, she knew that her mother would tell her that she had been day dreaming again. Bernadette placed Book back on the shelf and followed her mother into the kitchen. She helped her prepare the supper, after supper Brendan went upstairs to play on his computer and Bernadette and mother went into the lounge to play cards. They very rarely played cards now with Brendan not since Bernadette's amazing continual triumphs at cards when they had all three played together. Nowadays Brendan always stayed away from the mention of card games. Wist was mothers favourite card game, Bernadette's Patience which she often played by herself in the days before she had brought Book home from the library.

Mother and her played two games of Wist then the phone rang, it was for mother her friend Iris. Iris was a woman who had lost her husband like Bernadette's mother around the same time. Since those days they had become very close friends sharing days out together. They chatted about hair appointments and the latest gossip in the salon. Brendan came down from upstairs mother explained to Iris she would continue the call upstairs on the extension in her bedroom she then said to Brendan "you and Bernadette must not stay up watching television too late I'm going to have an early night" she then called out goodnight to Bernadette and Brendan. Brendan came into the lounge told his sister Oliver Twist was on the box and could they watch it, surprisingly to Brendan there was no argument from his sister's side she simply replied "Okay". They both watched the story of Oliver Twists birth unfold the wretched death of his poor beggared mother and poor baby Oliver being left in the arms of cruel wicked persons in a workhouse orphanage where love and care were forgotten. Captivated by the TV story unfolding eagerly they carried on watching. The depiction of history's face passed before them as they were shown scenes of Victorian London. A world where numerous poor peoples lived in such dark and blackened hovels the so called dwelling places of the poor and unfortunate whilst in a street around the corner there were candle wick lamps glowing from various windows of whitewashed walls beautiful in comparison to what they had just seen, where the rich lived.

It seemed quite unbelievable that the Victorian world they were seeing was so clearly divided between the haves and have-nots. How could you live in one street where peoples were clothed in velvets and furs and on leaving your cosily lit whitewashed home you turned the street to be met by street urchins, their clothes ragged and torn begging the price of bread so they would not starve. But Bernadette and Brendan watched with disbelief as people did just that and carried on in their own little worlds. Thank goodness a gentlemen who thought with his heart saved Oliver from a life of crime and debauchery to which he would have desperately adhered to, to survive but Oliver Twist was saved. The children remained fastened to their seats until Oliver Twist finished and it was time to go to bed. Bernadette and Brendan exchanged opinions of Oliver on the stairs before saying goodnight to each other and retiring to their bedrooms. Darkness now filled the lounge in the darkness and silence Book heard the distinctive cough of The Emperor awaiting his nights audience. Book looked further on down the bookshelf and came to Voices stirring and getting ready to deliver her chosen rendition of songs for the night. Book called her and asked did she know God Bless The Child by Billie Holiday she did and gladly obliged Book by singing so crooningly. Voices songs rang out into darkness of the lounge over the early hours until dawn broke through. In the morning Book heard mothers footsteps on the stairs mother came down the stairs to prepare breakfast for the children. Book had come to recognise all the steps of the inhabitants of the house, the light quick footsteps of Bernadette, the slow plodding footsteps of Brendan and now Book had become quite accustomed to the timetable of events in the house. After breakfast Bernadette came into the lounge she reached up took Book down from the bookshelf and placed her down upon her lap. She opened Book and began turning the pages she wanted to find the page with the forest she came to it.

She stared into the page and as she did so the greenery of the forest became a green mist, it began to cloak all the trees, Bernadette carried on staring into the green mist it was so hypnotic. Then the mist began to rise from the Book towards Bernadette surrounding her in a full haze of green mist then Bernadette's eyelids began to feel so heavy, they closed. Just then all was stopped by a noise at the lounge door and the green mist that had been surrounding Bernadette vanished. It was Brendan at the lounge door as he spoke Bernadette suddenly awoke from her hypnotic sleep, he said to Bernadette as it was Saturday would she come into the garden and play football with him she said she would. She placed Book back on the bookshelf and left the lounge. Out in the garden the early summer sun shone mildly down. Bernadette surveyed the garden, in the front half mother and the two children had planted flowers and herbs this part was out of bounds for all ball games, the children played ball games in the second half. Both children now looked down onto the flowers and herbs they had planted with their mother in early spring of last year. The lavender gave off a wonderful scent Bernadette then cast her eyes on the pink and red roses the bluebells and daffodils. Brendan pointed to the chives and sweet basil in the herb garden remarking to his sister how fine it all looked. Yes the sunlight had certainly cast her warm rays throughout for now in the garden all the colours had woven together throwing a tapestried carpet of colours into the air. Brendan now headed down to the other end of the garden Bernadette followed, both children loved the early summer. Bernadette ran into the sun towards the ball Brendan had kicked. Brendan in the past erected a makeshift goal with Bernadette in goalie he was able to practice his shooting kicks. Bernadette knew she could never replace her father but at least she was someone for Brendan to practice with. Now Bernadette said she was quite worn out and she wanted to go back into the house, Brendan said "okay sis" he was now going for a bike ride. Bernadette entered the lounge walked over to the bookshelf and took Book down from the shelf and sat in the green chair, finally after turning a few pages her eyes came to rest on the page with the forest. Again as she became hypnotically entranced her eyes staring deeply into the forest the green mist began to rise from the page and surround her, in this helpless trance like state again she felt herself being pulled into the forest and in this state could hear the Spirit Queens voice calling her, her eyelids began to feel heavy and close.

When Bernadette next opened her eyes she was standing beside a great stone wall, this wall what was it? She asked an old man passing by "Why" he replied "this is the great wall of Jerusalem behind it lies the old city." Bernadette stood and looked up at the great stone wall, it was so magnificent and maybe five or more meters high, she now turned and looked in front of her, the wall seemed to go on and on as far as the eye could see, she walked slowly taking in all the sights before her eyes then she heard a voice calling. "Alms for the blind, alms for the blind," an old man sat huddled on the floor before her shaking a tin. She searched inside her pockets but before her fingers got there her mind reminded her it was empty, panic now came upon her. Although Bernadette knew she was standing outside the old city of

Jerusalem she was in a foreign land with no money, she suddenly thought of home what would mother and Brendan be thinking, they had probably called the police by now and reported her missing.

She looked down at the blind man he had to help her, as she bent down towards the blind man she heard a cat cry in the distance a cold shiver ran down her spine. Feeling desperate and frightened she told the blind man she was penniless and would need money for a bed for the night. The blind man told her that he would help her but before taking the money from the tin she must listen to him. He told her that behind the stone wall lay the old city of Jerusalem and that the inhabitants had sometimes very old and different customs and that she was to take heed lest she lose her path and destination. Within the city walls before he was blinded he told her he had seen such sights and delights but he then paused and in a more serious tone he said to Bernadette beware of temptation. He told her again to take heed and added once inside the city walls ask for The Jewish Quarter for once you are inside the city walls you will need people that speak and understand your mother tongue. Then the blind man told Bernadette to take money from the tin, Bernadette bent down towards the tin and heard a cats cry again. The cat cry then stopped now a voice spoke, Bernadette had never heard the voice before, the voice said **"PICK UP ONE COIN OF GOLD AND YOU WILL GROW OLD."**

Bernadette now hesitated she most certainly did not want to grow old but shelterless in a foreign land she also needed the gold coin. Bernadette remembered after watching a programme about the homeless trying to survive on the streets how awful it was so she decided she definitely did not want to be alone on the streets in this foreign land. When Bernadette turned around the sight that greeted her was one of surprise and total amazement. Instead of the old blind man sitting huddled clutching his tin he had completely vanished into the air now all that remained on the stone floor was the tin. Bernadette heard the cry of a cat again as she bent down to pick up the gold coin, then a voice rang out into the air, again the same words **"PICK UP ONE COIN OF GOLD AND YOU WILL GROW OLD."** Bernadette took a step back and began to think again. In the attic of her mind she remembered the programme she watched about the homeless alone on the streets at night and the awful terrors and perils that happened to them, yes there was no question of weighing up the pros and cons her safety was more important than anything she stepped forward and bent down towards the tin. When Bernadette placed her hand in the tin to her surprise there were three gold coins, she was tempted to pick up three for three were more than one, the gold coins sat there gleaming sparkling all asking to be picked up. Bernadette decided yes I'll need more than one on my travels, two I'll pick up, then she thought a bit more, I don't want to be caught short anywhere so I'll pick up all three, just as she was about to put her hand in the tin she heard a cat cry, the words of the blind man came to her, **beware temptation**. Bernadette bent down and picked up one gold coin from the tin, she felt her face, her skin felt the same as before no wrinkles but what did those words mean?

Standing tall she walked ahead looking for a gate in which to enter the city wall. The wall of the city seemed to lead on forever and the stone path under her feet was rough not like the smooth paths back home. Her legs grew tired her feet heavy still she had not come to a gate opening in the city walls.

The sun was now setting and the evenings cloak of darkness began to unveil, darkened shadows started to appear on the walls, Bernadette began to feel a little scared and cold. Finally just up ahead of her she could hear peoples voices they were not speaking English she felt more lost than ever now, trying to communicate verbally was no good she started to feel desperate. Realising that these people were also trying to help her Bernadette now starts to use her hands and also facial gestures asking where she is. After much gesturing with her hands and face finally an old women comes out of the small crowd to help her. She speaks in broken English she tells Bernadette "You are at Jaffa gate this is the Arab section of the city, walk through Jaffa Gate into the Arab section of the city and carry on walking down the main street then when you come to the end of the main street turn to your right keep to your right always and then you will walk into the Jewish quarter where they can speak English like you, you will be safer.

Bernadette enters in through the big stone walls thanking the old women and waving farewells to the other people. As soon as she enters Jaffa Gate the sights, sounds and smells overwhelm her. Even though the sun is almost set still many stall holders and young urchins are on the city streets, voices hollering into the dusky air telling of their wears on their market stalls. So many tables with brightly coloured fabrics laid out, as Bernadette continues to walk amongst the various market stalls she catches sight of inlets behinds the stalls where precious gems and ruby's gleam beckoning her, and men come out from these jewelled dens with glistening gems necklaces bracelets in their hands telling her to try them on. Enraptured and mesmerised she travels on taking in all these magnificent sights. Next to one stall lays an array of the most exquisite, beautiful coloured fabrics asking to be picked up. An old woman watches Bernadette as her eyes fall on the gold leaf fabric, the old woman calls to Bernadette "Come come" she is pointing inside her shop to a makeshift changing room and a long mirror where next to it hangs a rich dark velvet ruby cloth. Bernadette feels inside her pocket for the gold coin she touches the coin then steps over towards the woman just as she does so a cat cry rings out into the air. Then she remembers what the old blind man had said about taking heed once inside the city walls lest you lose your path and destination.

Bernadette looks all around her the sun has now settled down for the night, her face fading on the horizon as she sinks lower and lower, Bernadette can see people hollering out their wears and young children milling around. She hurries on through the market stalls now not looking at any of the tempting wears, she now looks straight ahead of her, her eyes and feet leading her to the Jewish quarter. She quickens her pace through the hollering voices until she comes to the end of the main street, now what was it the old woman said, oh yes now turn right so Bernadette turns right. Ahead of her as she travels she can no longer see the street filled with market stalls, no longer human voices jamming and cramming the air, shouting out their wares. Now the air is calm she carries on walking through the calmness, Bernadette breathes in and looks around her, it feels like she has entered into a different world.

Now she can see clearly the landscape that lays before, her big whitish stones line the walls, this must be the Jewish quarter. Ahead of her she can see a large oak door amongst the wall of white bricks then she hears the cat cry again. There are words in the cry that call out in the wind **"STAY ON THE STREET THERE WILL BE DANGER AND COLD, WALK THROUGH THE OAK DOOR AND YOU WILL GROW OLD"** then the cat cry is gone.

 Bernadette certainly didn't want to grow old but the cat cry had said this before when she had taken money from the tin and then she hadn't grown old. She also definitely did not want to stay on the street in a foreign land where she knew she was far from streetwise, she also knew as darkness fell and the sun was no longer seen on the skyline it would grow cold. Bernadette took a deep breath braced herself and walked towards the oak door.

 Standing in front of the huge oak door she begins to feel scared hesitant her hands shaking she knocks on the door. Waiting Bernadette begins to tremble she thinks of her mother and Brendan then she thinks of running away but her feet seem rooted to the ground. There comes the sound of shuffling feet from the other side, slowly the large oak door creakily opens. There stands a frail old woman when she raises her head to see Bernadette's face the old woman's face is pale and wizened and she has these piercing fiery eyes. Sharply her eyes scrutinize Bernadette. The old women's eyes search Bernadette all over from top to toe then these eyes searched into Bernadette as if searching the meaning of her presence. Then the old lady asks Bernadette what she wants "I'm a stranger in this land and want shelter for the night" Bernadette splutters out in fear. The old woman looks Bernadette up and down again, seeming satisfied with Bernadette's appearance then says kindly "come in child you are welcome." Bernadette steps in through the great oak door once on the other side she immediately puts her hands to the skin on her face, her fingers searching out for lines and wrinkles but thank goodness there is no change as she has not grown old but what did that cat cry mean? Once inside she gazes all around her she is standing in a large rectangular shaped room. Over in the center of the room

lay a large wooden oval shaped dining table and around it tall inviting wooden chairs. Bernadette desperately felt like slumping down into one of the chairs, her legs and feet felt like lead and her whole body cries out for sleep but she remembers she is not at home and waits for the old woman to speak. "This is the dinning room where the meals are served, your breakfast will be served here in the morning from 8am to 9am, up those stairs are the sleeping quarters," Bernadette glances over to the stairs the old woman continues " you will find on the board in the dormitory prices for bed and breakfast, we don't serve evening meals." With that she bid Bernadette goodnight and left her standing in the dining room then she turns back and says, "When you climb the stairs and reach the top you will see a sign directing you to the girl's quarters they are on the right from the stairs, the boys are on the left."

Bernadette now stood alone in the dining room her feet felt sore, her body ready to drop all she had to do now was gather up enough energy to climb those stairs and fall into bed. Before turning to climb the stairs she surveys the room once again, over in each corner of the room stands two tall iron stand candelabras with eight candles on each, alight and casting shadows all around but Bernadette can not take all her surroundings in right now, with a sigh of total exhaustion she turns and climbs the stairs. She slowly picks her legs up, with each step she takes her legs ache, her whole body aches. She finally reaches the top now standing on a small landing she gazes around her, a candle on the wall sheds light down the hallway. She can now see a large arrow in front of her and painted underneath in black lettering is the word girls, the black arrow is pointed to the right. Bernadette feels nervous she is in a strange house, in a strange land she thinks of her mother and Brendan but her whole body cries out for bed. She follows the arrow along the narrow passageway the candle light guiding her, eventually she comes to a door that says girls, she turns the handle and creeps in quietly. Inside it is dark except for the moons light that shines in through the window. Bernadette is grateful for that. Girls in all beds were in slumber Bernadette began to search for an empty bunk, finally in the far corner she sees one. As quietly as possible she creeps towards it, the top bunk was occupied by a mousey brown haired girl snoring away Bernadette normally couldn't stand snoring but she was so tired she didn't care. She plonks herself down on the lower bunk lays back and nestling her head into the pillow falls asleep.

When Bernadette opens her eyes again its morning and all the girls in the dormitory are washing and dressing for breakfast, some bleary eyed entering in and out of the bathroom. Bernadette realises she has no wash things with her she has to go into the bathroom and brush her teeth with her fingers and comb her hair with her fingers. Bernadette stretches her legs gives out a final yawn climbs out of bed and heads for the bathroom. Once inside she yawns into the mirror gazing at her profile, she indeed looks exhausted, travel worn and red eyed. She splashes cold water on her face and sets about washing. Finished washing she heads back to the dormitory, all around her girls are discussing their travel plans. Bernadette now dressed and headed down for breakfast. When she arrives in the dining hall most folks had either eaten very quickly or skipped breakfast completely for the room was deserted. Bernadette approaches the dining table and sits down to have breakfast. The old woman appears that had greeted Bernadette the night before from a door behind the dining table. The old woman carries what seems to be Bernadette's breakfast on a large wooden tray. Silently she lays dishes before Bernadette and hurries back through the door. When the old woman has left Bernadette stares at the food in front of her, it wasn't like breakfast at home cereal toast and tea. In one dish lay fresh tomatoes sliced in another bowl what looked like a white type of yoghurt in another some sort of cheese and in a straw basket some type of flat bread that she had never seen before, she tried it, it tasted delicious. Then she made a sort of sandwich firstly layering slices of tomatoes on the bread followed by a top layer of cheese, as she sunk her teeth into it her taste buds were in complete ecstasy it tasted so scrumptious. Thirsty she looked for water and there further on down the table she spied an earthen ware jug and a clay beaker, when she put the water to her lips it was cold and tasted so good she drank and drank. Then she returned to the milky white yoghurt pudding, again her taste buds went wild with delight then Bernadette heard bells ring in the distance. She looked on the table at the empty bowls the breakfast had been so delicious and now she felt happy and full. She now decided she would venture out and explore her surroundings. She stood up from the table and like at home she collected the bowls, jug and beaker and placed them back on the wooden tray then left. Outside in the street she again hears a cat cry, then a bell begins to ring. She follows the ringing until she comes to a grey stone building, Bernadette would not have noticed it and passed it by for it was set into the walls if it had not been for the bell ringing.

She stops in front of the grey stone building and looks up. There on two grey stone columns sit two magnificent stone lions, their eyes staring deeply hypnotically into Bernadette's beckoning her inside. She then sees a great stone door underneath the columns where above the stone lions huge and stately survey their domain. Through the portico Bernadette enters inside. Once inside the bell stops ringing and Bernadette is surrounded by darkness. Through the darkness a faint light shows up ahead of her, walking slowly towards the light she feels a sudden chill and hears a cat cry three times. She has now reached the end of the passage, the candles shines more brightly now looking around her it seems she is standing in a hallway. To her right up ahead of her lay three doors. She approaches the first, a plaque on the door reads **WEALTH** she turns the handle and enters. On entering the room she gasps with delight for the walls around her are covered in such rich velvets and the floor beneath her feet marble with intricate exquisite gold mosaic tiles. At the end of the room sits an old woman on the most fantastically furnished chair Bernadette has ever seen, the chair like the walls is fabricked all over in a rich deep ruby coloured velvet and the arms of the chair are solid gold. The woman lifts her head to Bernadette and speaks "I have furnished my room in the most expensive lavish materials yet now I hear minimalism, bareness is the thing. Now I will have to strip my room bare and start all over again oh when will it ever end oh when will it ever end" Bernadette left the old woman bemoaning the state she was in turned the handle of the door and left.

Bernadette now looks around her and sees the plaque on the second door she moves closer to read it. The plaque on the wall reads *EGO* Bernadette turns the handle and enters. When Bernadette enters again she sees that all the walls around her are wallpapered in photographs, as she gazes around the room all the walls are prepared in photographs from the walls at the beginning of the room to the walls at the end. At the end of the room an old woman sits in a chair fabricked again in photographs. As Bernadette draws closer staring at the old woman sitting in the chair she see's that the photographs covering the chair resemble the old woman's face when younger she then again looks around the walls and realises the photographs on the walls are of the old woman. Bernadette then approaches the old woman sitting in the chair the old woman speaks to Bernadette "These are pictures of me you see, of course I am so beautiful you cannot but admire me" Bernadette agreed with the old woman although her face now bore marks of age and time you could see that indeed she had once been very beautiful. However Bernadette also felt sad for this old woman seemed to have forgotten that beauty was also found on the inside people thinking with their hearts not just beauty on the outside. She left the old woman and approached the door to leave but before turning the door handle she turned to the old woman and said "Beauty is not only skin deep dig deeper and you will find human hearts of beauty" then Bernadette turned the door handle.

Once again in the hallway she approaches the third door the plaque on the door reads **SEEKING HAPPINESS,** Bernadette turns the handle and enters. The room is bare there is no wallpaper or fabricked wallpaper on the walls. In fact the room is totally barren of any furniture or objects save for an old woman sitting on a plain worn old wooden chair with a fabric tapestried seat now very worn faded and threadbare. The old woman looks up at Bernadette and speaks, it was the most woeful voice Bernadette had ever heard she says. "I seek happiness but what's the point in trying to achieve happiness, I did not create it so it should be there for my taking I'm so so unhappy" then the old woman begins to sob and sob. Bernadette then replies to the old woman amongst her sobs "Happiness is there but its not in the air for your taking it is you and only you can create it" the old woman has now stopped sobbing and is staring at Bernadette then a bell rings, both stop and listen the bell continues to ring the old woman says to Bernadette "You had better go now." Bernadette turns the door handle and leaves, in the corridor the bell is still ringing Bernadette walks as quickly as she can amongst the semi darkness back to the great stone door. When she travels through the great stone door the bell stops ringing. Her surroundings are huge flagstones that repeat one after the other and all around her are rows of stone walls. At first she is unsure which direction to take but as her eyes search along one stone wall she sees an opening so Bernadette follows along this wall which finally leads her into some sort of square where she comes across a group of men dressed from head to toe in black robes.

Bernadette stops at the corner of the square and watches, some sort of ceremony is taking place curiosity drives her nearer. Now closer to the men in the black robes she can see before her an old church building which these men are entering into and coming out from. Some of these men carry tall round white candles that are smoking into the air giving out such wonderful smells. Suddenly a voice speaks close to Bernadette she turns around and behind her sits the blind man. Bernadette cannot believe it last time when she turned to speak with him he had vanished into the air now he was back again, she stands there rubbing her eyes to be sure and when she looks again yes it is the blind man alright. As she approaches him he speaks **"In there is a book of the world of lifes light read by many only some have sight."** She listens to the blind mans words and turns back to the blind man to ask him more once again he has vanished into the air as if he had never been there at all then Bernadette hears a cat cry. The scene in front of her begins to blur she rubs her eyes again and again, the scene before her is fading she wants to stay, to stay in this world to find out more but her body is being pulled by a very powerful force, her eyes begin to feel heavy and close. When she next opens her eyes she is back at home in the green chair. Book lay on the floor at her feet, outside she hears the sweet singing of a lone bird. Bernadette lies back resting into the chair, the house so silent Brendan must be out with his friends and mother shopping. She gazes out of the lounge window Bernadette had to tell Brendan what had been happening to her she had to tell someone. She hoped Brendan would hurry home soon and mother return Bernadette sat back in the green chair and gazed upon the book.

    She thought of all the strange happenings that had taken place since she had bought the Book and taken it home from the library. Then she heard a key turn in the front door oh great Brendan's home but instead it was mother. She entered into the lounge and seeing Bernadette in the green chair said "Oh your not still in that chair with that book Bernadette you've been there all morning" before Bernadette could answer her mother carried on. "Brendan's gone out to play football with his friends when he came in you were snoozing and he didn't want to disturb you. Look Bernadette I've got to pop back out to the supermarket I forgot the eggs tell Brendan I'll be home soon and please Bernadette go out for a walk and get some air its not good for you lounging in the house all day. Bye darling be back soon". With that the front door slammed and mother was gone. Bernadette looked into the lounge she felt bored she wanted someone to talk too. Then she bent down and lifted Book up from the floor casually she leafed through the pages then she came to the page with the forest, again the green mist began to rise from the Book surrounding Bernadette pulling her into the Book. Her eyelids began to feel heavy and close.

Enlightenment

When Bernadette opens her eyes again this time she is not back in the old city of Jerusalem but in the forest where she had first met the Spirit Queen. The trees stand tall before her then suddenly she hears a little boys laugh. Bernadette looks to the left of her nothing but forest trees and on the forest floor she spots a forest beetle busily at work. She looks up to the right of her nothing, the laughter must be ahead of her, she steps forward. With each step the laughter grows louder and louder, it now rings with a second voice, a young girl's laughter too. As Bernadette stumbles forward she walks into a sort of clearing, the scene that greets her amazes and astonishes her. Set out in front of her in a semi circle are these high-tech computers, their outer casings are all see through you can see the body workings of these computers amazing!, Brendan certainly did not have a computer like this! Sat at two were a young boy and small girl, Bernadette stays hidden under the branches of the large oak tree, the children are too engrossed in their computers to notice any strangers. The boy then turns to the girl "Come on see this game its wild," the young girl picks up her chair carrying it in the boys direction Bernadette's eyes follow her. The little boy then speakes to the girl "Want to play a game with me?" the young girl nods. On the screen is a game with characters resembling people, together they watch the screen as the boy explains that they can make a film, the young girl gasps with delight. The young boy

explains more to the girl showing her pictures of all the characters they can have in the film, there was a sly old man who had a wicked grin a young boy and girl, their mum and dad, the young boy said "wicked" the young girl "cool" and there were a few other characters. Then he changed the screen and showed her a choice of sounds they can make. The girl turns to the boy and says "This looks brilliant let's make a film" "Okay" replies the boy.

As Bernadette remains hidden under the branches of the large oak tree she watches the children playing on the computer. As the game unfolds the children totally involved in choosing characters, sounds and scenes for the film, Bernadette watches on. She notes the whole activity requires a lot of effort, focus and imagination on the childrens part, it reminds her of when Brendan and her played on his computer at home. Everything was set up in the programme it was then left to the children to choose scenes and sounds. When the children press the sound key to go with the cliff scene in the film they want sounds of waves splashing on the shore but also a continual rolling sound. After much searching of sounds in their computer they finally find one. The children make a short film then finish, it was exiting and scary especially when the young boy was pushed by the sly old man towards the edge of the cliff but his dad saves him. Bernadette smiles when she thinks of the future, computers and literature together working alongside each other. The little boy turns to the young girl and says "Stay and watch this game you'll love it". Bernadette watches the children their eyes follow every action on the screen.

The young boy sits there in front of the computer his fingers twitching impatiently waiting to push the keys whilst the girl sits waiting for the next action. The game he has now chosen seems to be about discovering hidden treasures placed in many parts of the world, good geography learning skills Bernadette thinks as she looks on. There is a really fit man and woman in the game who are a team. The part of the game that is hardest is overcoming various obstacles, it could be crocodiles in a swamp ready to eat you or climbing up a pyramid. As the children watch with delight and amusement this team travel across walls up and down pyramids and into stone darkened passageways that are really creepy. Now and again the boy lets the girl push the keys now she's got the hang of it, to the boys delight the girl is even faster on the keys then he was, a major part of winning the game was how fast you could press the keys so that the characters in the game were in control and could overcome all obstacles placed in their way. The boy now leaves the little girl in control of the game as she is able to deal with situations the women and man find themselves in. It is as if the computer had totally entranced the children for they were still unaware of Bernadette's presence. The game now finished the boy and girl turned to one and other and sang **"We love computers their really great, press the right keys then the computers our mate"** then they both laughed and hugged each other.

Bernadette now stepped out from under the great oak when she had nearly reached the forest floor the boy must have heard Bernadette's feet. He turned around he didn't look very different from Brendan except his hair was brown the boy stared at Bernadette's green eyes. "Hello my names Bernadette", the little boy acknowledged her greeting with a warming stare. "I'm sorry to interrupt your games I was just curious about something and wanted to ask you a few questions about it, do you mind?" Bernadette thought of the Spirit Queen then asked the children "Do you like playing computers a lot?" the little girl started to giggle. "Why yes of course" replied the boy. "There great for playing games on and learning things, we love them." Just then it was as if the computers had heard the boys words for they all made a loud whirring sound that echoed throughout the forest. "But what about books" asked Bernadette. "You know The Hungry Caterpillar The BFG and Peter Pan In Never Land", the young boy looked at Bernadette and said "Story books are okay but we love computers." Just as the Spirit Queen had said story books did not seem to have an important role in the future, Bernadette slowly walked around the semi circle eyeing the computers. As she stood there gazing at the computers she felt a force pulling her she knew now what the force was, it was time for her to go, her eyelids began to feel heavy and close.

Farewell

When she awoke she was back in the forest and the Spirit Queen was waiting on her toadstall. "Good day Bernadette how did you find your travels?". "So many strange things happened" said Bernadette. "There was this old derelict house, a young boy, a balloon ride in the sky where we met Peter Pan, Tinkerbell The BFG and you. Then I travelled to the Old City of Jerusalem where I met a blind man there, I then entered three strange rooms where there were three old woman.

There was a voice and a cat cry in the voice that kept on saying I would grow old but thank goodness I didn't. Then finally I travelled to a forest a bit like this one where I met two small children playing on computers". "Well Bernadette said the Spirit Queen the cat cry with the voice that said you would grow old meant not with wizened skin but old with wisdom through your travels. As I told you on our first meeting story books when read are a guiding force bringing alive the spirit of the book and at the same time the books spirit voice, for do not forget authors of these books whether alive or deceased are brought alive when a book is opened. Computers are excellent tools to the written word however they still are only machines, they do not possess the human spirit, the human imaginative mind. Humans created technology, computers were invented by man to aid them in the future, however a future world without books would be barren especially a world without story books. People of all lands, future generations will be lost without the guiding force of books." Bernadette then replied "Through my travels I've learnt how much the child values indeed cherishes story books, the young boy in the derelict house pined after his friend the BFG and then when I travelled into the forest and found two children playing on computers I learnt about their love of computers.

Then changing the subject she asked the Spirit Queen "but how did you know about the derelict house Jerusalem the blind man the cat the three old women and the children in the forest with the computers." The Spirit Queen replied "I was with you all the time on your travels, watching you and guiding you. Now you have entered the spirit world and awoken me I will always be with you Bernadette. Bernadette there is also something very important I must tell you about books. Not all books have a good human voice, human spirit inside them. Once the book is opened the spirit inside comes to life, however if it is a bad human spirit it will guide the person in evil ways. I have prepared a potion of good spirits in this green bottle I wish you take it back with you to your world. You will never need it to protect you for you have strong good spirit inside, you read books often so your spirit's energy is renewed every time you read. All humans have an individual spirit inside them but many do not read now with the computer world so actively used, so many human spirits have become weak. This bottle provides a top up of good human spirit. To use it successfully pour it into a bath and let the person in trouble bathe in the spirit of goodness. Say these words and look at the bottle **Spirit Queen, Spirit Queen please, please come to me, fill up the bottle and set the spirits free.** Through your travels Bernadette you now know the troubles of the book world and its future if the present state of things continue in your world. Bernadette we have to say farewell now and you must return to your world to fulfil this crusade for the book world." The green mist began to rise, Bernadette could feel a force pulling her, she knew it was time to go. Her eyes began to feel heavy and start to close but she no longer struggled to keep them open.

Finally Home

When Bernadette finally awoke she was back in the green chair, in her left hand she was holding the green bottle that the Spirit Queen had given her in the forest and Book lay on her lap. She began to think upon all her travels and experiences. The use of story books in the future and this generations love of computers and technology. Then she gathered up all her thoughts that had been tumbling about in her mind and placed them in some order. She thought of the places where books mainly lived, libraries,schools and a minority of habitats, the home. What role could these places play in, in the future? Oh Yes Publishers as well, books are found in abundance in these places. She remembers on her visits to the local library there was a class of school children there who arrived with their teacher, they then entered the childrens library. Bernadette thought on this event, she remembered a boy and a girl had gone straight to the computer instead of the bookshelves, other children gathered around but they were told by the teacher to come away from the computer and go to the bookshelves. Bernadette thought more on this, the way forward surely for the future was to join story books with technology. The world had started to do this in technology with I-pods but technologies compatibility with books was not recognised as of great importance and relevance in this society for the future generations now and to come. All places where books abound could do a lot more, the corridors of learning, schools for instance could do a lot more for this place was where some children got their first taste of books. Yes schools could do a lot more and local libraries also needed to do a lot more to introduce children to the bookworld and maintain encourage the children's enjoyment. Yes that's it get the children so involved in stories then the rest will follow.

Bernadette then gazed down at Book on her lap. So it was true the Book did hold magic powers, Bernadette thought more on her adventures. It was very clear now that without story books the spirit world would die and so would the Spirit Queen. If there were no story books there would be very little imagination or adventures, no make belief, how boring the future would become. Just then Brendan came in from the garden. "Bernadette come out and play." "In a minute" replied Bernadette. "Your always reading those story books I don't know why you don't get a job reading them when you grow up". That was it Brendan had given her a great idea, I now know what I shall do when older, I'll train as a childrens librarian. Oh I do love you Brendan she thought she could hear Brendan calling out her name from the garden she rose put Book back on the shelf and went out into the garden. Bernadette looked at Brendan and said "I'm sorry I'm here now what do you want to play?" "Basketball" came the reply, Bernadette threw the ball smiling all the time she felt so happy as she ran up the garden out of Books view. Book knew her life was finally beginning and in future days and years to follow the book world would be treated with the honour and importance it deserved. Book settled herself down but not before having a gaze around her in case any of the books were free to talk. She chose the right side of the bookshelf where she knew her friends were placed. Looking along the shelf she could see The Emperor talking to himself but Book didn't want that kind of conversation. Voices was humming a tune but she had just been travelling so she wanted to talk about it, luckily she found Gulliver free. "Had a pleasant time said Gulliver once Book caught his gaze, I saw you being put back on the bookshelf by Bernadette" "I had a really interesting time" replied Book "I've taken Bernadette on some travels in my story book although they were different travels to you Gulliver they were still of the same topic, mankind and the future but my travels focused on the book world and the future for the book world. I'll talk to you more about it in depth Gulliver another time but right now I feel like celebrating". Then Book turned in Voices direction.

Lightning Source UK Ltd.
Milton Keynes UK
UKOW041154081112

201860UK00001B/89/A